OUR LITTLE ATHENIAN COUSIN OF LONG AGO

This edition published 2026
by Living Book Press
Copyright © Living Book Press, 2026

ISBN: 978-1-76183-146-1 (hardcover)
         978-1-76183-145-4 (softcover)

First published in 1913.

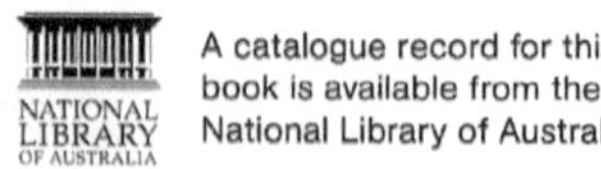

A catalogue record for this book is available from the National Library of Australia

Our Little Athenian Cousin of Long Ago

by

Julia Darrow Cowles

.HIERO.

CONTENTS

Preface

As Rome is associated in the minds of all with military heroism and power, so Athens is associated with art. The story of *Our Little Athenian Cousin of Long Ago* has for its setting the reign of Pericles, 444-429 B. C., when Athens was at the zenith of her power and glory, and when art and architecture reached their climax.

The story has been purposely made to emphasize the artistic, rather than the political, side of Athenian life, since it is through its art that Athens has most powerfully influenced our own life and times.

Every care has been taken to make the story a vivid portrayal of the civic and home life of a child of the time, while adhering strictly to the best authorities in regard to detail.

Pronunciation of Proper Names

A-crop'o-lis

Ag'a-thon

A-pol'lo

A'ri-ad'ne

Ar'te-mis

A-the'ni-an

A-the'ne

Ath'ens

Cal'li-as

Chlo'ris

Ci'mon

Cle'on

Crete

Cri'to

Da'mon

De-me'ter

Di'o-nys'i-us

Do'nax

Du'ris

Eu-phron'i-us

Har-mo'ni-a

He'ra

Her-mip'pos

Hi-e'-ro

Ho'mer

Il'i-ad

I'ris

Lys'i-as

Ma'nes

Med'i-ter-ra'ne-an

Me'los

Men'o-do'ra

Mi'nos

Min'o-taur

Nep'tune

Ni-car'e-te

O-lym'pi-an

O-lym'pic

O-lym'pus

Pal'las A-the'ne

Pan-ath'e-næ'a

Par'the-non

Per'i-cles

Pei-si'stra-tus

Phid'i-as

Phi'lo

Phor'i-on

Pi-ræ'us

Pȳth'i-as

Py'thon

Rhodes

Soc'ra-tes

Spar'ta

The'ron

The'se-us

Tro'jan

Vul'can

Zeus (zus)

CHAPTER I

The Guest-Friend

More than twenty-three hundred years ago two travellers, richly dressed, and mounted upon donkeys, made their way slowly along the narrow and irregular streets of Athens. They were followed on foot by a group of slaves, who carried huge bundles in which were blankets, clothing and cooking utensils, showing that they had journeyed from some distance.

The travellers were Phorion, a famous Grecian architect, and Duris, his son, a boy of twelve years.

Presently they stopped before a house in the Street of the Sculptors, and one of the slaves rapped loudly upon the door.

"I believe this is the house of Hermippos," said Phorion.

"I do not see how you can tell," replied Duris. "They all look exactly alike to me." And he glanced up at the wall of the house, which was close to the street. There were windows in the upper story, but none in the lower. A single door relieved the bare face of the lower wall.

All the houses up and down the street were built in a similar way.

Before Phorion could answer there sounded a sharp rap upon the inner side of the door to warn them that it was about to be opened, and the slaves stepped quickly to one side so that, in swinging outward, the heavy door should not strike them.

A slave appeared in the opening, and Manes, one of the slaves of Phorion, approached him.

"My master, Phorion," said Manes, "has come from a far distant island and is worn with the long journey. His family are guest-friends of your master's family. In token of this, here is the broken ring which is the sign of their treaty. The other half of the ring is in the keeping of your master."

The slave took the broken ring, bade the two guests enter, and went to seek Hermippos.

Duris looked about him at the furnishings of the court of the house in which they waited. There were chairs, couches and tables about, and all were of simple materials, but artistic in shape. The lamps, of which there were a large number, consisted of an open vessel for oil in which a wick was placed, and all were beautiful in form and in workmanship.

Several rooms opened from the court, and presently

from one of these stepped Hermippos, the sculptor. He was a tall man of fine appearance, and Duris liked him at once. But Duris was even more pleased at sight of a young boy of about his own age, who followed Hermippos.

"Ah," he said to himself, "now I shall have a fine time during my stay in Athens. I did not know that Hermippos had a son."

Greetings were exchanged between the two men, and Duris was introduced to Hiero, the son of Hermippos. Hiero was a fine specimen of an Athenian boy, and as Duris looked into his manly, attractive face, he felt that his own visit to Athens had taken on new interest.

The two artists were soon busily engaged in discussing the buildings and sculptures of Athens.

"Pericles is doing wonderful things for the city," said Hermippos. "He is a successful general and a wise and unselfish ruler. But he is a lover of art and of beauty as well, and he has determined that Athens shall be made the most beautiful city in the world."

"I am very anxious to see the Parthenon," said Phorion, "for I understand that it is the most magnificent temple ever built."

"It is," replied Hermippos earnestly. "I shall be glad to take you to see it. I thought it an honor to make some of the statues which are upon its walls."

"I, too, have been honored by Pericles," said Phorion, "for he has sent for me to plan a great music hall, which he is about to build."

"That is an honor, indeed," replied Hermippos. "We must visit the Acropolis to-morrow, and you, of course, must pay your respects to our ruler, Pericles."

In the meantime the boys, Hiero and Duris, were becoming acquainted also.

"I am glad you have come," said Hiero frankly. "We will have some good times together." And then he added: "I shall want to hear all about your journey from the Island. I never have travelled, but I have often wished that I might."

"I like to travel," replied Duris, "except when the sea is rough," and at that he made such a wry face that they both burst into hearty laughter.

"I am glad we are guest-friends," exclaimed Hiero. "I wonder when the treaty was made between our families."

"I understand," replied Duris, "that some of our ancestors fought together in battle a great many years ago and became much attached to each other. So they agreed that when any of my ancestor's family visited Athens they should be your guests, and when any of your ancestor's family visited our home they should be our guests. So they took a ring which one of them was wearing and broke it in half. And the broken ring has been passed down from father to son, and is kept as a token of the family treaty."

"That is very interesting," said Hiero earnestly, as Duris finished his story.

The custom which Duris had described did not seem at all strange to Hiero, for in that far distant time inns were few and small, and were far from being comfortable. Neither did the fact that Duris and his father had come unexpectedly surprise him, even though their visit was likely to prove a long one, for railways, mail service, telephones and the telegraph had never been heard of, so there was usually no way of knowing when a guest was to arrive until he presented himself at the door. But the people of Greece were kindly and hospitable and often cared for strangers who were not guest-friends.

"Tell me about your journey here," urged Hiero, for by this time the boys had begun to feel like real comrades.

"We journeyed first on foot," began Duris, "for it was some distance from our home to the seaport. The slaves, of course, carried our blankets and food, for we were two days on the way."

"It must have been like a long picnic!" exclaimed Hiero.

"Yes," said Duris, "it was fun, though by the end of

the second day the walking grew tiresome. We had travelling shoes studded with nails. I liked eating out of doors, and it was pleasant to sleep under the stars.

"But to me," Duris continued, "the most interesting part was the sea voyage. The ship we were on was a trireme."

"I do not know much about ships," said Hiero. "What is a trireme like?"

"It is called a trireme because it has three banks of oars," replied Duris. "The slaves who row the ship sit in banks on each side, and there are three banks at different heights. There was a captain of the slaves who played upon a flute to mark the time, so that all the oars struck the water at the same instant.

"It was very rough one day, and I felt pretty bad, for the motion of the boat made me ill, but I managed to get out in order to watch the oars. I was not too ill to wonder whether the slaves could keep their even stroke, for the wind was churning the water into great waves."

"Well, did they?" asked Hiero.

"No," replied Duris, "for once the slaves had a rest. But I was well repaid by the sight I saw, for the master of the ship had had two great sails hoisted, and the ship was being carried forward by the force of the wind."

"My!" exclaimed Hiero, "I should like to take a trip like that!"

"We left the ship, of course, when it reached the Piraeus, which is the seaport of Athens, as you, of course, know. There my father hired donkeys on which we rode to your city."

"How did you like the Piraeus?" inquired Hiero.

"It is a fine place," said Duris. "The streets are straight and quite broad; not at all like the streets here in Athens. I should think a person would get lost here, unless he knew the city well."

"I suppose he might," said Hiero with a laugh, "but I am so used to the city that I never had thought of that."

"The walls which extend from the Piraeus to Athens are wonderfully big and strong," added Duris.

"Yes," said Hiero. "They are sixty feet high, and broad enough for two chariots to be driven side by side upon their top. No army can ever break through those walls, and so Athens can never be cut off from the sea.

"There is to be a great festival this year in honor of the goddess Athene," continued Hiero, "and I hope that we may visit the Piraeus together, for the festival ends with a regatta upon the water."

"That ought to be a fine sight," exclaimed Duris. "I hope we may be here for the festival."

CHAPTER II

IN THE MARKET-PLACE

"Come, Duris," called Hiero after breakfast the next morning, "Father says that we may go with him to the market. Later," he added, "we are going to the Acropolis. That, you know, is the hill that you must have noticed as you passed through the city yesterday. On it is the Parthenon, which Pericles, our ruler, has built. It is the most magnificent temple in the world. Near the Parthenon is a statue of Athene, which is forty feet high and is made of ivory and gold."

"Oh," exclaimed Duris, "I caught sight of the statue, I think, as we came into Athens. Father told me that it was made by the sculptor, Phidias, and that he is the finest sculptor that has ever lived."

"That is true," replied Hiero, "and there are many of his statues and carvings in the Parthenon also. But, oh, the Parthenon itself! I can't tell you about it, but, somehow, when I look at it, I just seem to feel how beautiful it is. All the artists and architects and sculptors say that it is perfect.

"But now," Hiero added, with a little laugh at his own enthusiasm, "we are going to the market. That is not so beautiful as the Acropolis, but I think you will find it interesting."

Hermippos and Phorion were now ready. With them were quite a company of slaves who were to attend them upon the street. Among these were Philo and Theron, pedagogues of Hiero and Duris, for every Greek boy of good family had his slave, who was called a pedagogue. This slave attended him wherever he went and was responsible for his good behavior.

Slaves also attended the men of Greece, not only to wait upon them and to carry for them any articles that might be needed, but also to show the standing and the wealth of their owners. So it was quite an imposing little company that left the home of Hermippos.

The streets of the city were narrow and ran in all sorts of irregular directions, as Duris had said. They were not graded, and in many places there were steps leading to higher or lower portions of the city. There were no sidewalks at all. People walked in the streets, and were careful not to keep too close to the houses lest a door should be hurriedly opened and strike them.

"We will go first and buy provisions for the home," said Hermippos, as they drew near to the market-place.

"And we are just in time," exclaimed Hiero, "for the bell of the fish market is ringing." People were now hurrying in the direction of the fish stalls, for fish was a favorite food of the Athenians.

All about the market-place were booths and shops where articles of many sorts were sold. There were also altars and statues, and marble seats, for the market was a general gathering place. Here the men of the city met to visit; here travellers came, to bring news from a distance; here business was carried on; and here the public affairs of Greece were discussed.

"Look!" exclaimed Hiero to Duris, and he pointed to one of the fish stalls.

"There is a fight!" said Duris.

"It is only a pretence," laughed Hiero. "See, in a moment one of the fellows will fall. Then the owner of the stall will throw water upon him to revive him—but the fish will be better drenched than the slave. That will make the fish look fresher, and they will sell better. But," added Hiero, with a comically solemn expression, "it is against the law to water the fish—except, of course, in case of accident."

"Oh, I see," laughed Duris. And a moment later he added, "There, it has happened exactly as you said!"

"Look this way," said Hiero, suddenly pointing in another direction, "here comes a procession of soldiers.

It is the bodyguard of Pericles, the ruler of Athens. You will see him soon."

Duris jumped up on the marble seat, that he might see over the heads of the men about him.

The citizens saluted their ruler, and shouted as he passed, for he was a favorite with all the people. No other ruler had done so much for the good of the citizens or for the beauty of their city, and the Greeks loved beauty as no other nation ever has done.

"Hurrah!" exclaimed Duris, as he jumped down from the seat. "I am glad that I saw him! I am proud to think that he sent for my father to build one of the new temples."

As the boys reached a part of the market between two columns Hiero pointed toward the Acropolis. "See," he said, "what a good view of Pallas Athene we get from here. But the statue can be seen, of course, from all parts of the city, so the goddess guards us well."

The Greeks, like the Romans, worshipped many gods. They believed that the home of the gods was in Mount Olympus, a great mountain far to the north of Greece. Zeus was the ruler of Mount Olympus, and dwelt in a magnificent temple. Here he summoned the other gods into council whenever the affairs of men were to be considered.

The gods often quarrelled among themselves, and acted very much as the Greeks themselves did, but still they were supposed to have power over the earth and the sea; over the crops of the farmer and the battles of the general; to guard the homes and lives of citizens; and to rejoice in the many festivals and games of the people.

Every occurrence in nature was traced to the action of some god. Zeus was said to drive the chariot of the sun in its daily course through the heavens; Vulcan to forge the thunderbolts; while Demeter watched over the fields of grain. Iris was the rainbow, and Neptune the god to whom the sailors prayed, for he had power to grant them a quiet voyage.

The Greeks did not worship their gods because they were better than themselves, but because they were more powerful.

The many stories of the gods, which we call myths, but which formed the religion of the Greeks, were so full of poetry and of imaginative beauty that people of every nation love to hear them, even though they do not believe in them in the same way that the Greeks did.

But we must remember that Hiero and Duris believed these stories of gods and goddesses to be literally true, and so the great statue of Pallas Athene on the Acropolis represented to them a living goddess who protected Athens, and for whom the city was named.

CHAPTER III

THE ACROPOLIS

"Where are the boys?" asked Hermippos of Phorion, as they were about to leave the market-place.

"I think we will find them in yonder crowd," replied Phorion. "I see Philo and Theron near by."

As they stepped to the booth where the crowd had gathered Hermippos listened for a moment and then laughed.

"We will have to wait," he said. "Lysias, the merchant, who has just returned to Athens with a ship-load of goods from the Island of Rhodes, is telling of an encounter he had with pirates who tried to seize his vessel and rob him of his cargo. We cannot expect the boys to be interested in the Acropolis till that tale is finished."

"Surely not," replied Phorion with a smile.

"But fortunately," they heard Lysias saying in a shrill voice, "a ship from the Island of Melos came to our rescue, and the pirates were driven off. And now, my friends," he continued, "I am here to show you the beautiful goods—"

"Come, boys," said Hermippos, touching Hiero upon

the shoulder, "I think you have heard all of Lysias' story that you would be interested in."

The boys turned quickly and made their way through the crowd. "Did you hear Lysias tell of his fight with the pirates?" asked Hiero, with sparkling eyes, as he joined his father.

"I heard a part," replied Hermippos. "There are pirates enough on our seas, to be sure," he added, "but I think Lysias is not above inventing the story in order to draw a crowd about his booth. It is an excellent way to sell his goods."

The boys looked rather foolish for a moment, and then Hiero exclaimed with a laugh: "Well, I don't care. It was a good story, anyway!" And to this Duris heartily agreed.

But even pirates were forgotten when the boys reached the top of the broad marble steps that led to the Acropolis. Duris was eager to see the temples and statues of which he had heard so much, and Hiero was quite as eager to point them out to him.

A love of beauty was part of the Greek nature. It was to them like the fragrance of flowers or the warmth of the sunlight. Perhaps Hiero and Duris thought even more than most Greek boys of their age about the beauty of carvings, and statues, and temples. Both their fathers had taught them of these things all their lives.

The Parthenon was all of pure white marble. It was surrounded by fluted columns, which were simple, strong, and perfect in outline. All about the building were beautiful carvings showing a procession in honor of Athene, such as took place in Athens every four years. This was the festival of which Hiero had spoken to Duris. The Parthenon was built in honor of this goddess, who was called by the Romans Minerva. She was the Goddess of Wisdom.

Inside the temple there were many other carvings and statues, and Hiero pointed out with pride those which his father had made.

"Let us sit down for a time," said Phorion, "and look carefully at some of these groups of statuary. See," he said, turning to Hiero and Duris, "here, over the front of the Parthenon, is a group which tells us of the origin of Pallas Athene. Duris, can you tell us the story which it represents?"

Duris flushed a little, but he did not hesitate, for every Greek boy was supposed to know the stories of the gods and goddesses. These were among the first stories which their mothers told them as little children.

"Pallas Athene," began Duris simply, "was the daughter of Zeus. She sprang from his head, fully grown, and clad all in armor. The gods were astonished at the sight, and the earth and sea were shaken. Athene is the Goddess of Wisdom. She inspires men to defend their homes and their cities. She teaches women the arts of spinning and weaving."

"That is very well told," said Hermippos, as Duris finished. And then he added: "At the farther end of the temple we noticed another group of figures showing the conflict between Athene and Neptune. Hiero, can you tell us of that?"

"I think so," replied Hiero. "It was when Athens was first built, and had not yet been named. Both Athene and Neptune wanted the honor of naming the city, so the gods decided that the one who should create the most valuable gift for the people should give the city its name and guard it.

"Neptune struck the earth, and there sprang forth the horse. Then Neptune explained how powerful and strong the horse was, and how swiftly it could carry their men into battle.

"The people applauded Neptune, and declared that nothing more useful or more wonderful could be given them. But when they had ceased praising Neptune, Athene touched the ground, and an olive tree sprang up, with leaves and fruit.

"Then Athene explained to them that the fruit would

yield them food and oil; the trunk would supply them with material to build their homes, and with fuel to keep them warm; the leaves would give them grateful shade; and the tree itself was a symbol of peace and prosperity, while war would cause bloodshed and sorrow.

"Athene's gift was seen to be more wonderful and more valuable than Neptune's, and she was chosen to rule over the city, and to give it her name."

"That is good!" exclaimed Phorion. "I am glad to see that you boys understand the old Greek stories and can tell them so well. Now," he added, "I think we will all enjoy better seeing the great statue of Athene for having heard these stories told again."

Duris gazed in wonder as he stood before the image of the goddess, while Hiero called his attention to its details.

"You see," he said, "all the flesh is made from ivory, and the drapery is of pure gold. And look at the eyes. See! the pupils are of jewels."

"What does the smaller statue, which she holds in her hand, represent?" asked Duris.

"That is the statue of Victory. Athene's shield and spear are in her other hand. Notice, too, the serpent coiled at her feet. The serpent, you know, is a symbol of wisdom."

"It is a wonderful statue," said Duris. "I hope that I may sometime see Phidias, the sculptor."

Duris Gazed In Wonder As He Stood Before The Image Of The Goddess.

"You are quite likely to," answered Hiero, "for he visits the Acropolis often."

"You are fortunate to be in Athens this year," said Hiero, as the little procession at last turned toward home. "The festival of Athene occurs only once in four years. The frieze in the Parthenon shows you what the procession will be like. I am glad we can see it together."

"So am I," responded Duris heartily.

As they turned into the Street of the Sculptors he asked: "When does your school begin?"

"In two days," replied Hiero. "I hope that your father is planning to send you, too."

"What sort of master have you?" inquired Duris.

"Oh, he is good to the small boys," said Hiero, "but the rest of us have to mind our ways, for he is rather fond of using the cane."

"Well," said Duris, with a laugh, "I'll risk the cane, for I, too, hope that I am to go to school in Athens."

CHAPTER IV

PREPARING FOR THE FESTIVAL

Hiero's mother, Harmonia, belonged to one of the noblest families of Greece. She was famed for her beautiful handiwork, and she had taught Helen, her older daughter, to embroider as beautifully as she herself could do. So it came about that Hiero's older sister, Helen, was chosen as one of the girls who were to embroider a magnificent robe for the goddess Athene. Every fourth year a new robe was made, and during the celebration of the festival of Athene it was presented as an offering to the goddess.

Of course nothing was too beautiful, or too costly, or too elaborate for this gift to the goddess who ruled over Athens. The most expensive materials were chosen for the robe, and silks of richest colorings were used to embroider it, as well as threads of silver and gold. Only the best needle-workers of the city were allowed to work upon it.

Athene was the goddess who presided over the art of needlework, and so the young girls of Athens offered prayers to her daily, that their handiwork might be worthy of a place on the robe. Very happy and proud were those who were selected to do the work.

The figures embroidered upon the robe represented a great battle which was once fought between the gods and the giants, and it is only when we remember that the statue of Athene was forty feet high that we can understand how it would be possible to embroider such a scene upon her robe.

Hermippos was well pleased when he learned that his daughter Helen had been awarded so great an honor.

"My sister is an artist, as well as my father," declared Hiero laughingly.

There was one more in the family of Hermippos to be interested in the wonderful robe, and that was Chloris, the younger sister of Hiero. Chloris was ten years old, while Helen was fifteen.

Perhaps you wonder why neither Helen nor Chloris had joined Hiero and Duris in their visits to the Acropolis or to the market-place, but this was a liberty never allowed to a girl of good family in Athens.

The girls never went out upon the streets except upon some special occasion, when they were accompanied by slaves belonging to Harmonia. They were never allowed to stand in the doorway that looked out upon the street. They might look from the windows in the second story of the house, if they did not go close enough to be seen by people in the street below.

The girls did not go to school, for the schools of Athens were for boys only. Their mother taught them at home all that a girl of those days needed to know. She taught them to spin and to weave, to sew and to embroider. She also taught them how to read and write, and how to play upon the lyre and sing. And this was much more than was taught to many of the girls of Athens.

From their earliest years they were told the stories of gods and goddesses, for this, as we have learned, was the religion of the Greeks.

When members of the family were alone they ate their meals together. Hermippos reclined upon a couch, and Harmonia sat upright at his feet. The younger members of the household sat upon chairs. Each one was furnished with a small table, upon which food was placed by the slaves.

When there were guests in the house Harmonia, Helen, and Chloris had their meals served in their own rooms, for the Grecian women did not mingle with men, except with those of their own family. In every Greek house certain rooms on the upper floor were set apart for the use of the women.

The women of Athens sometimes visited at the homes

of relatives or friends, but not often, and when they went upon the street they were always accompanied by female slaves.

In some of the religious festivals, however, the women were allowed to take a part, and in the festival to Athene, which would soon occur, they carried a part of the offerings, and formed a very beautiful part of the procession.

It is no wonder, then, that Harmonia and Helen were now full of eager plans, for their life had, usually, so little of change or pleasure.

Chloris still played with dolls, of which she had several. One was a rag doll, and one was of clay painted in bright colors. One doll, which she especially loved, had movable arms and legs, and clothes which could be taken off. This doll had a bed, and a two-wheeled cart in which Chloris drew her about. Chloris called her Athene, and on the days of the great festival Chloris intended to have a play festival in the court of her home, for her doll. So while her sister worked among the older girls upon the magnificent robe for the goddess, Chloris sewed and embroidered busily upon a robe for her doll. She did the work just as carefully and as beautifully as she could, for before it would be time for another festival she would have put away her dolls, and, quite likely, would be thinking of getting married. Most Athenian girls were married between the age of fourteen and sixteen, and Chloris looked forward to this as a matter of course.

Her cousin, Nicarete, had been married the winter before, and Chloris had been very much interested in all the arrangements. Nicarete had played with and sewed for her dolls until she was obliged to give them up to help her mother and the maids prepare the clothing which she was to wear as a bride.

When this time came, Nicarete collected her dolls, with all the beautiful garments that she had made for them, and in the care of slaves she went to the temple of the goddess Artemis and there laid her girlhood treasures upon the altar. She offered a prayer to the goddess, and then returned home to prepare for the new life in her husband's home.

Then beautiful garments were made, and there was much excitement in the usually quiet rooms of the women's apartments. Nicarete often wondered what her husband would be like, for she had seen him only twice and then at public festivals. The marriage had been arranged by her father and his.

Chloris had gone to the wedding and she remembered the sacrifices that were offered to the marriage gods and the great feast that followed.

At this feast all the guests, both men and women, ate

together, but the children were served apart from their elders, and with simpler food.

She remembered how pretty Nicarete had looked in her bridal clothes, with the veil, and ribbons, and flowers in her hair; and how Hiero had gone about among the guests, bearing proudly a basketful of cakes, and singing: "I fled from misfortune; I found a better lot."

Chloris had been away from home so few times during her life that this wedding had made a great impression upon her, and she had had weddings for her dolls many times since then. She wondered how she would feel when she should have to carry her dolls to the temple and leave them upon the altar, as her cousin Nicarete had done.

"It will be very exciting, I am sure," she confided to her doll, Athene, as she sewed upon her robe, "and I hope my husband will be a great artist, like my father."

CHAPTER V

At School

"Now for school!" exclaimed Hiero, as he and Duris left the house early in the morning, their pedagogues, Philo and Theron, following them as usual.

"We go to the grammar school in the morning," Hiero explained, as they walked along, "and to the wrestling school in the afternoon. I am doing my best in wrestling and running, for I am looking forward to the Olympian games. I hope sometime to enter the contest for boys."

"That will be fine," exclaimed Duris, with sparkling eyes. "You ought to run well," he added, looking with admiration at Hiero's strong, graceful figure.

"Not better than many others," replied Hiero modestly. "But one would hardly hope to win in the first race he entered."

"It is well worth trying for, at any rate," responded Duris. Then, with a laugh, he said, "Look at the boy yonder, on stilts. He manages them pretty awkwardly. I think he is likely to have a fall."

"He surely will," said Hiero, laughingly, "and he is likely to be late at school."

"What is this?" asked Duris, as they came upon a group of boys standing about an old man who was seated at an angle of the road.

"Oh," said Duris, "it is a street school. The master is not very well fitted to teach, and he cannot afford to hire a room, but people who can pay little send their boys to him and he teaches them out of doors. I suppose they find it better than no school at all."

"I should think it would be difficult for the boys to keep their minds upon their lessons," said Duris.

"I should, too," responded Hiero, "but you see they have chosen a quiet street corner, where there is not likely to be much excitement."

"O-ho!" Hiero exclaimed, a moment later, pointing to the house they were passing. "My friend Cleon lives here, and I see by the wreath upon the door that he has a new brother."

"Ah," said Duris, "we have the same custom of hanging a wreath upon the door when a boy is born, in the Island. And do they wrap bands of wool about the door posts, in Athens, when a girl is born?"

"Yes," replied Hiero. "I suppose that is because the girls must spin and weave."

"Here come some of the younger boys of our school," said Hiero, dodging as he spoke, for the boys were running rapidly, and rolling hoops as they ran. The hoops had small bells set inside the circle and the bells chimed merrily as they were rolled.

The schoolroom which Hiero and Duris entered was plainly furnished. It had a seat for the master, and benches for the boys. Each pupil had a waxed tablet, upon which he wrote with a stylus. The sharp end of the stylus cut the letters in the wax; the flat end rubbed the wax smooth after the lesson was finished.

The master read to the pupils from the poems of Homer, and the boys wrote the lines on their tablets. Then they read the lines aloud, and afterward committed them to memory.

Homer was the greatest of the Greek poets. His best known poem was the Iliad, which told of the Trojan War. Though this poem was composed more than twenty-five hundred years ago, it is still one of the most wonderful poems ever written, and people to-day enjoy it just as much as the people of Greece did at the time that Hiero and Duris were going to school.

Some of the older pupils could repeat nearly the whole poem, for it aroused the enthusiasm of every Greek boy. It told of a great war between the Greeks and the Trojans, or people of Troy. This war lasted for nine years, and at last the Greeks were victorious.

The legends tell us that Homer, the poet who wrote the Iliad, was poor and blind. But he was a welcome guest wherever he went, for he sang his wonderful verses to the music of his lyre. Every host was glad to have such a singer entertain his guests.

One of the rulers of Athens, named Peisistratus, understood, better than any one else had done, the value of Homer's poems. He called together at Athens all persons who knew these poems, and he had them sing or recite them. Although this was long after Homer's death, his poems never had been written. They had been sung and recited year after year at festivals and gatherings of the people, and one person had learned them from another. Now Peisistratus had them written, in the form that had been given best, so that they should never after be forgotten or changed.

After that, many copies were made, each one written by hand on a parchment scroll.

So we may see why, in the schools such as Hiero and Duris attended, only the master had a copy of the poems, and the pupils had to write the lines as they were read to them, and afterward commit them to memory.

After the reading and writing the boys were given a

THE MASTER READ TO THE PUPILS FROM THE POEMS OF HOMER.

lesson upon the lyre, for at the gatherings and entertainments at their homes the men of Greece often sang and played for their guests. The boys at school were taught the best music as a very important part of their education. This was done not only that they might entertain guests, but in order that they might become gentle and quiet in manner. Then, too, the boys were taught to sing so that they could join in the choruses in honor of the gods, and that they might learn the war songs of the soldier, for the Greek army sang whenever it went into battle.

The boys of the wealthier families in Athens did not expect to earn their living, or to take part in the business life of the city when they were grown, nor did their parents expect them to do so. Their time would be given to political and social affairs; to an enjoyment of art and music; and to the beauties and pleasures of life. If there should be war, many of them would go as officers or soldiers, but the every-day work and trade of the city was left to slaves, or to citizens of the poorer class, who were looked down upon because they must work for their daily living.

"Father," said Hiero, as the boys entered Hermippos' studio after school, "I had a pretty warm argument with Euphronius, at school, to-day. He taunted me by saying that you worked with your hands, as the potters and trades-people do, while Duris' father thought of marvellous plans for buildings, but had slaves to cut and lay the stones."

"And what reply did you make to him?" asked Hermippos with a smile, yet flushing a little.

Phorion, who was present, showed his interest also in Hiero's reply.

"I told him that you thought of such beautiful carvings and statues that you could find no one with skill enough to work them out for you."

"Very good!" exclaimed Phorion heartily. "I think this Euphronius you speak of could find little to say to that." And then he added more seriously: "Surely it is only the thoughtless and the ignorant who can confound the work of a sculptor with that of a potter, or a maker of sandals."

CHAPTER VI

THE WRESTLING SCHOOL

To have a strong and beautiful body was considered by the Greeks almost as important as to have a well-trained mind; so every Greek boy was taught to run, to jump, to throw, and to wrestle. There were separate schools in which the boys were trained in all these exercises. We would call such a school a gymnasium, but in Athens it was called a wrestling school.

Duris had found that he could read and write quite as well as Hiero, and he could play upon the lyre even better, but as they were on their way to the wrestling school he said, "You will be far in advance of me in running and wrestling, I know, for I have had no training in gymnastics. Of course," he added, "we boys had contests of our own on the Island, but we had no teacher. My pedagogue, Theron, taught me to read and to write, and my mother taught me to play upon the lyre, but I have had no training in running or wrestling."

"There is to be a contest in jumping in the school this

afternoon," said Hiero. "You will be interested in that. Some of the boys can jump a remarkable distance."

The wrestling school consisted of a large open court, around which was a covered portico, divided into small rooms and halls. Duris looked eagerly about him. A large number of boys were already in the court. One was just mounting a horse. There were no stirrups, and he used his lance to help him vault to its back. In another part of the grounds a young man was practising spear-throwing. But these boys were older than Hiero or himself.

"Come," said Hiero, touching his arm, "they are getting ready to jump."

Duris stood aside with a group of boys while Hiero took his place among the contestants.

A line was drawn upon the ground, crossing a small mound. One by one the boys who were to take a part in the contest ran from a distance to this line, and then jumped from the mound.

Duris exclaimed at the length of the jump as the first boy came lightly to the ground. A young man ran forward and drew a line to mark the distance.

Hiero was the second to jump, and his mark was in advance of the first.

"Surely no one can do better than that!" exclaimed Duris to one of the boys standing near him.

"Oh, you just wait and see!" replied the boy. "Hiero is not a great jumper. But when it comes to running! Well, they talk about his being a contestant at the games some day. You should *see* him run!

"Look! Here comes our greatest jumper now. It is Cleon. Be prepared for a surprise."

And Duris was surprised. It seemed to him as though the boy before him must have wings, for he seemed truly to fly through the air from the mound, and the mark that he made was so far ahead of all the others that the difference itself would have been a creditable leap for one who had had no training.

A great shout arose from the boys, and Duris joined it heartily.

"That is what training does!" exclaimed the boy at his side.

"But have the others had less training?" asked Duris.

"Perhaps not," answered the boy, "but Cleon has practised jumping more than any other exercise, and there is no one of his age or size who can begin to leap as far."

When all the contestants had taken their turn, the length of each jump was measured with a long chain, so that a record could be kept for each pupil.

After that there were exercises in running, and in quoit throwing. Duris became more and more interested, and when a torch race was begun, he himself took part. This race did not require so much speed as it did skill in keeping one's torch lighted while running, and at this Duris, to his own surprise, did remarkably well.

"You will enter the regular classes to-morrow," the master said to him, as he and Hiero were about to leave, and though Duris knew that he would fall far behind his companions at the start he determined to make the most of his training and to gain strength and speed as fast as possible.

Phorion was given a glowing account of the wrestling school that night. When Duris had finished, Phorion said, "I am glad you are to have this training. But do not forget to seek grace and symmetry, as well as strength and speed. Let me show you what I mean," and he led the way into Hermippos' studio.

Lifting the cloth with which it was covered, he pointed to a magnificent statue which Hermippos had that day completed.

"This," said Phorion, "is a statue of Theseus attacking the Minotaur. Do you boys remember the story?" he asked, for Hiero was also in the studio.

"Tell it to us, Father," said Duris, "even though we have heard it before."

"Very well," said Phorion, seating himself, while the boys stood respectfully before him.

"Many years ago," he began, "the city of Athens had to pay tribute every year to King Minos, of the Island of Crete. This yearly tribute did not consist in money, but in seven of the fairest youths and seven of the fairest maidens of the city. They were taken in a ship to the Island of Crete, where they were devoured by a terrible monster called a Minotaur. This monster had the body of a man and the head of a bull.

"At the time of our story the King of Athens had a son named Theseus, who was as brave as he was strong and beautiful. When the time of the yearly tribute came near, Theseus declared that he was ready to go to Crete as one of the victims of the Minotaur.

"The people begged him not to go, but he was determined, and perhaps something in his face or manner told them that it was best to let him have his way. It might be that some good would come of it.

"When the ship arrived at Crete, Theseus, as the king's son, demanded that he be allowed to see King Minos.

"As he stood before him, he said: 'Oh, King, I have come to pay the tribute of my city. But as the son of my royal father, I ask that I may first meet the Minotaur alone.'

"King Minos laughed scornfully at Theseus, but he could not refuse his demand, so he sent him forth to meet the Minotaur, and promised that his companions should speedily follow.

"But while King Minos laughed at Theseus, the king's daughter, Ariadne, determined that she would help him. She admired the brave youth, and she knew of the magic means which would enable Theseus to overcome the Minotaur.

"Ariadne followed him when he left her father's palace, and promised him her help. She told Theseus that the Minotaur was not only strong and powerful, but that he lived in a winding abode, called a labyrinth, from which no one ever could find their way back. But she promised to give him a sword which was a magic weapon. 'If you can but touch the Minotaur with it,' she said, 'his strength will leave him, and you will have no trouble in killing him. But,' she added, 'before you enter the labyrinth, you must fasten this cord just outside and unwind the ball as you go. Then, when you have killed the Minotaur, you can follow the cord back, and so reach the entrance to the labyrinth.'

"Theseus thankfully took the sword and the ball of cord, and did as Ariadne had told him. He reached the Minotaur, and a terrible struggle followed, but at length

Theseus thrust the magic sword into the Minotaur's body, and slew him. Then, following the cord as Ariadne had directed, he made his way back to the opening of the labyrinth. Hastily summoning his companions, they once more boarded the ship and sailed away to Athens.

"Never, after that, did Athens have to pay tribute to Crete, and the memory of Theseus is honored in Athens to this day.

"This figure, as you see," added Phorion, "represents Theseus attacking the Minotaur, and the reason that I brought you in to see it just now is that you may study the figure of the young hero. You will notice how Hermippos has shown his strength by the powerful muscles, and by the manner in which he stands. But that is not all that makes the figure so wonderfully good. It is the grace of the figure as well as the strength; the perfect development of every part of the body, not of one particular part. Do you understand what I mean?"

"I think I do," responded Duris slowly, while he looked earnestly at the marble figure before him.

"Then," said Phorion, "you will understand what I mean when I tell you that I want you to think no more about the distance you can run, or jump, or throw a quoit, than you do about the manner in which you run, or jump, or throw. I want you, in other words," concluded Phorion, "to make your body graceful, symmetrical, and strong: equally ready for the demands of art, or for heroic deeds."

Hiero and Duris looked for a long time at the figure of Theseus, and when they left the studio both felt that they understood the beauty of the sculptured hero better for having listened to Phorion's words.

CHAPTER VII
THE FESTIVAL

Many festivals were held in Athens, for the people loved the processions and games and contests. But there was another reason for them. Each festival was held in honor of some god or goddess, and so was intended to win their protection and favor.

Of all the many festivals no other was half so splendid as the one held in honor of Pallas Athene. This festival was held once in four years. It was called the Panathenaea, and the celebration lasted for many days.

As the time for it drew near, Hiero and Duris grew more and more eager.

Duris had now been in Athens nearly a year, and he had made fine progress in both the grammar and wrestling schools. He no longer found it difficult to go about the streets of the city, with their many turns. Almost every day he and Hiero went to the market-place, or to the Acropolis, where they watched the building of the music hall which Phorion had planned.

Hiero had told Duris all that he could remember about

the last Panathenea, and little else was talked of among the boys at school. Both Hiero and Duris were to take part in the contests this year—Hiero in the running race for boys, and Duris in the torch race. Four years before, Hiero had thought it wonderful to watch the great festival. Now he was proud and happy to think that he was to take part in it himself.

At last the great day came. Even Chloris was to see the procession, and she was placed under the care of trusted slaves belonging to her mother. Harmonia and Helen were to have a prominent place among the women who were to take part in the sacrifices, and in the great procession.

The first day was given up to musical contests. The chief event was the singing of a hymn to Apollo. This was sung to the music of the lyre, and the hymn told of the victory of Apollo, the god of music and of light, over the Python, which represented darkness.

There were choruses of men's voices; and poems were recited to music.

Judges called the name of the winner in each contest, and he received a sum of money, while a beautiful wreath of gold was placed upon his head.

"Of course the music was fine," said Hiero, as he

and Duris returned home, "but I can scarcely wait for to-morrow."

The boys were up the next morning before daylight, for the gymnastic contests began at sunrise. The first one was the running race for boys, and Hiero was to take part.

"Don't forget any of the rules," cautioned Duris, as he left Hiero, "and be sure to save strength for the final dash. I'll cheer you on with all my might," he added, "and I hope you'll win."

Hiero stood among the boys who were to enter the race, and oh! how he did hope he might win, so that some time he might be thought worthy to compete in the Olympic games.

The boys were soon given their places at the starting line; they took the position which had been taught them at the wrestling school, the signal was given, and away they darted. Each one put forth his best efforts, but Hiero remembered Duris' parting words, "Remember to save strength for the final dash," and within a few feet of the line he sped like an arrow away from the one boy who had kept abreast of him—and touched the goal.

How Duris cheered! And all the people cheered; while Hiero, flushed and happy, saw his name written, the first victor in the gymnastic contests. A prize would be given him at the close of the day.

The boys of the wrestling school crowded around to shake his hand, and wherever he went during the remainder of the festival, he was greeted with smiles and congratulations.

After the races of the boys, came those of the young men, and later, those of the older men. Besides running, there were wrestling and boxing contests, and it was several days before all were finished.

Then came contests of another sort, in which horses were used. There were horseback races, with spear throwing, and chariot races, in which four horses were driven abreast, hitched to a two-wheeled chariot. The driver stood upright, and a second man rode in the chariot. While the horses were running at full speed, the latter jumped from the chariot to the ground, and up again to his place.

Next came chariot races by soldiers dressed in armor; and then a dance by warriors with glittering shields, and spears, and helmets, who moved to the music of the flute, and at times sang a stirring chorus.

The torch race took place in the evening.

"Now," said Hiero to Duris, "you must show your skill in handling the torch. I shall cheer for you, and I expect you to win."

WITHIN A FEW FEET OF THE LINE HE SPED LIKE AN ARROW.

Duris laughed. "I will do my best," he answered, as he took his place among the torch bearers.

As the signal was given, each boy lighted his torch at the altar fire, and then they sped toward the goal—but not too swiftly, lest their flame should be blown out. It was a merry race, and a pretty one, too.

One by one the racers stopped, as their speed put out their flames, while others dropped far behind, hoping thus to keep their torches burning, and so win in the end.

Duris and another boy named Callias were in the lead. As they drew near the goal they were side by side. Still abreast, they had almost reached it when Callias dashed ahead. But the sudden dash put out the flame of his torch, and Duris, with his torch still burning, touched the goal.

Then it was Hiero's turn to cheer, and Duris' turn to flush with pleasure at the great shout that went up from all the people.

"Ah, we have each won a prize," said Hiero, as he grasped Duris' hand. "I am glad of that."

But the greatest day of the festival was yet to come. That was the day upon which the sacrifices were offered, and the great procession went up to the temple of Pallas Athene.

CHAPTER VIII
THE GREAT PROCESSION

The procession started at sunrise. Hiero and Duris, as victors in the races, were to march; Hermippos and Phorion would ride on horseback; and Harmonia and Helen were to carry offerings and garlands.

There were great preparations in the home of Hermippos, and all the household rose long before daylight. Even Chloris was not forgotten. She was placed in the care of some of Harmonia's most faithful slaves, who were to see that she had a good place from which to view the great procession.

The priests, who were to offer the sacrifices, took their places at the head of the long line. Then followed the foremost men of Athens, and after these the men from other states and colonies, who had been sent to do honor to the goddess. These bore offerings which were to be placed upon the altar.

After them came the younger women, who bore incense, and costly vessels of silver and gold, which were to be used when the offerings were made. Helen was among the younger women, and they formed a beautiful part of the procession. They wore garlands upon their heads and girdles to bind the graceful drapery of their garments.

Other women, carrying cakes, and fruit, and wine, for offerings, came after. Among these, Harmonia walked with dignity and grace.

Following these were the older men of the city, and then came the four-horse chariots with the drivers that had taken part in the races.

One part of the procession was made up of a great number of cows and sheep that were to be sacrificed upon the altar, and with them were the herders who kept them in order.

Then came the cavalry, with generals and soldiers on horseback; and private citizens riding fine horses that danced and pranced to the music of the fifes and citharas. Among this group road Hermippos and Phorion.

Following these were the soldiers on foot, and the victors in the contests, with Hiero and Duris walking side by side, and bearing themselves proudly, as victors should.

But the most wonderful part of the procession was the great ship, set upon rollers, so that it could be drawn through the streets. Stretched like a sail from its mast was the splendid robe which had been made for the goddess. The figures of the gods and the giants in their terrific battle had been so wonderfully embroidered that the whole seemed more like a great painting than like a piece of needlework. The people looked upon it in wonder, and felt that it was, indeed, an offering worthy of Athene.

The procession passed the market-place, moved slowly about the Acropolis, and then stopped at the foot of the broad, marble steps.

At this point, while all the people waited, the robe was taken from the ship, and then, as it was carried up the steps to the temple of Athene, the procession again moved forward.

Upon the altar which stood before the temple the women placed their offerings; the priests presented the animals as a sacrifice to the goddess; the new robe was brought forth and placed in the temple before the wonderful statue of the goddess, and the great pageant of the Panathenaea was ended.

Then the people formed themselves into family groups, and seated themselves here and there for the banquets which always followed the sacrifices. The meat of the animals offered upon the altar was divided among the people, and a great feast finished the chief day of the festival.

Two tired boys stretched themselves upon their couches that night, but before they slept, Hiero called, "Don't you dare to over-sleep, Duris, for you know we go, to-morrow, to the regatta at the Piraeus!" "Call me if you waken first," replied Duris; and in another moment they were both asleep.

The next that they knew there was the clatter of hoofs, the rumble of chariot wheels, and the shouts and calls of men in the streets outside.

"The people are already on their way to the Piraeus," called Hiero, springing up.

In a few moments he and Duris were eating a hasty breakfast. It had not taken them long to dress, for each boy had only to slip into a single garment, called a chiton, and he was ready for the day. The boys wore sandals upon their feet outside the house, but no hats at any time.

Their pedagogues were ready to attend them, and they soon joined the gay throng in the streets.

"This is the last day of the festival," said Hiero, "and we must make the most of it."

On the two great walls which connected Athens with its seaport were soldiers on horseback, chariots, and bands of musicians, all moving toward the Piraeus. In the wide space between the walls throngs of people on foot were pressing eagerly in the same direction. It was not an orderly procession, like that of the day before, but a great mass of pleasure-seekers, bent upon making the most of the last day of the festival.

The boys ran in and out among the people. Philo and Theron found it difficult to keep them in sight. The strange dress of the men from other states, the gay trappings of the soldiers, and the prancing of the horses, kept them looking first upon one side and then upon the other. Hiero was startled when Duris at length exclaimed, "Oh, Hiero, look! The sea!"

Blue and sparkling, the waters of the Mediterranean stretched away before him, as far as he could see. For a moment he stood quite still, enjoying the beauty of it. Then he darted swiftly down to the water's edge.

The harbor was filled with ships. Some were sailing slowly before a lazy breeze, while others were rowed briskly by hundreds of glistening oars.

The great bows of the ships, rising high above the water, were carved into the figures of gods or of heroes.

Presently the ships drew up into line. "They are getting ready for the race!" exclaimed Hiero.

After what seemed to the boys a long time, the signal was given, the oars of each ship struck the water together, and the race had begun.

It was a beautiful sight, and the boys watched it with breathless interest.

The crowds cheered as one vessel and then another led in the race. And when one ship came back into the harbor far ahead of the others, there was a great shout from all the people. The crew of this vessel were declared the victors, and were presented with costly gifts, after which a great feast was made for them.

When the race was over, the boys suddenly discovered that they were hungry. So they found a comfortable place upon the shore, and soon were enjoying the lunch which Philo and Theron had brought from home.

Late in the afternoon Hiero and Duris, tired but happy, returned to Athens.

"The big festival is ended," said Duris with a sigh.

"Yes," replied Hiero, "but in Athens there are festivals every month—though none quite so fine as the Panathenaea."

CHAPTER IX

HIERO'S UNCLE IS ILL

"My uncle is very ill," said Hiero, as he joined Duris a few mornings after the Panathenaea. "My father is going with him to the temple of the god of healing."

"We had a physician in the Island who came to see my mother when she was ill," said Duris. "Have you no physician in Athens?"

"Oh, yes," answered Hiero quickly, "but such wonderful cures are reported at the temple that my uncle wishes to be taken there."

"The physician who came to cure my mother," said Duris, "brought an orator with him."

"An orator!" exclaimed Hiero. "Why was that?"

"Because the physician was afraid my mother would not want to take his medicine. The orator told her how good the physician's medicine was for her trouble, and how many persons it had cured. He talked a very long time about her illness, and how it should be treated. When he had finished, my mother felt certain that the medicine would cure her. She took it, and was well again in a few days."

"That was good," said Hiero. "I hope the priests in the temple will do as much for my uncle."

"Will they give him medicine?" asked Duris.

"They will bathe him, and have him sleep in the open air on the porch of the temple. He will have warm sunlight, and breezes from the ocean. Then perhaps the god will tell him in a dream what he must do to be cured.

"I have been in the temple," Hiero continued. "It is filled with offerings brought by people who have been cured. There are models of feet and hands and arms, made from stone or wax; and there are cocks and other animals made from clay, which poor people have brought. But there are beautiful gifts, too: cups of silver, and of gold, and ornaments, and precious jewels."

Just then the boys heard steps close beside them, and turning, they saw Donax and Agathon, two old slaves of Hermippos.

"You were speaking of your uncle's sickness," said Agathon. "If I had anything to say about the matter I should send to the house of Crito for a drug which he alone knows how to prepare. It is made from a plant which grows near the top of a mountain. It is a certain cure for the sickness and pain which troubles your uncle."

"But cannot the priests of the temple tell my uncle of this drug?" asked Hiero.

"Bah!" exclaimed the slave. "The priests know nothing of it. It was revealed to the family of Crito many, many years ago, and it is known only to them. It is a secret cure," added Agathon, "but it is certain."

"The drug of Crito may be good," said Donax, the second slave, "but I have little faith in drugs. I would think it safer to send for our own slave, Menodora. She can drive away the disease by chanting and by the use of charms."

"How can charms and chants cure sickness?" asked Hiero.

"Ah," said the old slave, "they please the evil spirit who brings the sickness, so that he leaves the one who has been troubled. It is easy to believe," he added: "cannot the one who brings sickness take it away again?"

"Bah," exclaimed Agathon, a second time. "I have no faith in chants or charm strings, and I warn you that our master, Hermippos, would not thank you to teach such foolishness to these boys."

At this, both Hiero and Duris laughed. "Don't be alarmed, Agathon," said Duris. "I can match Donax' story with one of my own. A poor boy who lived not far from us on the Island was taken with terrible pains in his hip. One of the slaves ran to quite a distance to get a young puppy. He brought it home in his arms and laid it against the boy's bare hip. He said that the puppy would absorb the pain and his young master would be well. In an hour's time the boy was entirely cured, we were told. But," added Duris, "I forgot to ask whether the puppy showed signs of pain afterward!"

"Doubtless it did! Doubtless it did!" exclaimed Donax, shaking his head solemnly. "I have heard often of this treatment. It is very good indeed."

Hiero and Duris exchanged a smile at the old slave's faith, but Agathon gave vent once more to his favorite expression, "Bah!"

"But," said Hiero, earnestly, "there can be no doubt of the cures wrought in the temple. I, myself, have read the tablets. One tells of a dumb boy who went there with his father. They offered a sacrifice. Then the slave of the god asked the boy's father if he would promise that his boy would make a thanksgiving offering if he were cured within a year. And the boy answered, 'I will.' And after that he could speak as others do."

"And do you remember, Hiero," said Duris, "one tablet told of a lame man? A boy snatched his crutch and ran away with it, and the lame man sprang to his feet and chased the boy."

"Yes, I remember," said Hiero. "I should like to have seen that cure."

CHAPTER X

FESTIVAL OF THE BEAR

"I wish I were old enough to go hunting," said Hiero, as a young man wearing a broad hat and high boots passed along the street, followed by several hunting dogs.

"How odd he looks," exclaimed Duris, for usually the men of Athens went about with bare heads and with sandals on the feet.

"Yes," replied Hiero, "he does look odd. But he will find need for the high boots to protect him from brush and thorns."

"I wonder what he expects to hunt," said Duris. "I see he carries a javelin."

"I suppose he will hunt bear and make an offering to Artemis," said Hiero. "It will not be long before the festival of Artemis, and bear skins will be in demand for that, though I think there are few bears near Athens. Helen and Chloris are to see the feast," he added. "I don't care about the festival, of course; that is only for girls. But I would like to join the hunt."

"How do the men hunt, here in Greece?" asked Duris.

"They usually have dogs, as this man has," replied Hiero, "and the dogs are splendidly trained. The men have nets spread, and when the dogs find the game they drive it toward the net. Some of the nets are made in the form of a bag, which can be drawn up to hold the animal after it is caught. Other nets hang from sticks. When an animal runs into one of these the net falls and the animal gets tangled in it. Then the hunter can easily throw his javelin and kill it.

"The hunters often have to go through thick brush to follow the dogs to the game. Sometimes the brush is thorny. That is why they have to wear the high boots. I have a pet hare which father brought me. He caught it in a bag net one day while hunting. I soon tamed it and it eats from my hands. Would you like to see it?"

"Yes, indeed," said Duris; "I like animals. Father sometimes tell me that I should live on a farm. At home I had several pigeons, and a pet monkey that was up to all sorts of mischief.

"I have always wanted to get a peep into the temple of Artemis," continued Duris with a laugh, "for I have been told that a live bear is kept there."

"Perhaps it is true," responded Hiero. "You know the sign of Artemis is a bear."

But if the boys were not interested in the coming

festival of Artemis, the girls, Chloris and Helen, certainly were, and Chloris talked of it from morning till night. When Harmonia and the slaves grew tired of listening to her, or of answering her questions, she turned to her dolls. They never failed to listen quietly, no matter how many times she told them of the fun that was in store for her.

"You know," she began, one day, shaking her finger earnestly at the oldest doll, "that Artemis is goddess of the moon. Her sign is a bear. Wait and I will show you one."

Chloris looked among her treasures until she found the figure of a small bear, cut from stone.

Seating herself once more before her dolls, she continued: "This is a bear. See! It is the sign of Artemis. If you will listen I will tell you why.

"Once upon a time Artemis was changed into a bear. She had long claws and a growly voice and black hair all over her. And she walked on four feet, though sometimes she forgot and stood up straight. The reason she was changed into a bear was because the goddess Hera was angry with her.

"One day Artemis' son went into the woods to hunt. He didn't know his mother had been changed into a bear, so when he saw a bear in the woods he took up his bow and arrow to shoot it. But it was his own mother!

She couldn't talk and tell him who she was, but Zeus saw what a dreadful thing was going to happen, so, before the boy could shoot, he snatched them both away, and placed them among the stars in the heavens. Up there they are called the Big and Little Bears, and the tip end of the Little Bear's tail is the North Star.

"Artemis, you know," continued Chloris, "has a beautiful temple in the Acropolis, and every year she has a festival.

"This year," Chloris added, shaking her finger impressively, "I am going to the festival. Only women and girls go. We dress in bear skins and dance the bear dance around the altar in the temple. Then we have a feast and I shall meet other girls. Oh! I am so glad that there are some festivals that we girls can go to!

"Come," she suddenly cried, catching up one of the dolls, "I shall dress you as Artemis, and these little dolls shall be bears, and we will play festival, just as soon as I get you dressed."

CHAPTER XI
THE NEW SLAVE

"Father," asked Hiero one morning, "did I hear you say that you needed another slave?"

"Yes," replied Hermippos. "Why do you ask?"

"Because I saw Cimon bringing a number of slaves into the city yesterday."

"That is good," said Hermippos. "I must visit his market to-day."

"May Duris and I go with you?" asked Hiero.

"Yes, if you wish," replied Hermippos, and Hiero ran quickly to tell Duris to be ready.

They were soon on their way, with the usual number of slaves. The purchase of a slave was always an event to Hiero, but he thought no more about his father's buying one than an American boy or an English boy would think about his father's buying a new horse.

Every family had slaves, and even the poorest families had one. If any one had asked Hiero whether his father bought slaves, he would have answered, "Why, of course." And he would have wondered why they should ask such

THE SLAVES WERE UPON A PLATFORM WHERE THEY COULD BE SEEN BY THOSE WHO WISHED TO BUY.

a foolish question. But really there would have been no one to ask the question.

To the people of Athens, slaves seemed just as necessary as a house to live in, and they were bought and sold in much the same way.

When Hermippos reached the market he found it well filled with people. The slaves were upon a platform where they could be seen by those who wished to buy. Hermippos went among them, questioning one and another. Then he found Cimon, and pointed out one of the slaves with whom he had talked.

"He is a vase-maker," said Cimon, "and worth much more than the common slave."

"I am willing to pay somewhat more," replied Hermippos.

After a time a price was agreed upon, and the money paid. Then Hermippos and the two boys returned home, the new slave taking his place among the others who had attended Hermippos.

When they reached the house, and the door was opened, they were met by a shower of sweetmeats.

"What does this mean?" asked Duris, catching some of the falling sweets his hands.

"Oh," laughed Hiero, "it is the custom to scatter sweetmeats through the house when a new slave enters."

"Why do you do it?" asked Duris.

"It is a good omen," replied Hiero. "That is all I know about it, except that the sweet-meats are good to eat." With that he caught up a handful, and invited Duris to do the same.

"It is certainly a pleasant custom," exclaimed Duris.

"Yes, much pleasanter than another which we observe," Hiero responded. "Once a year we choose a slave to represent everything that is mean and worthless. Then the other slaves run after him, beat him, and drive him out of doors. That," Hiero added, seriously, "is to drive poverty and trouble away from the home."

"Do you remember seeing a slave run into one of the temples in the Acropolis yesterday?" asked Duris, after a pause. "I intended to ask you about it then, but you were talking with your father, and I forgot about it. The fellow looked frightened, and he ran as though for his life."

"He probably was running for his life. Some of the slave owners are terribly cruel. If a master goes too far the slave can run to the altar of some god and claim protection. I am glad my father is good to our slaves."

"When we left the Island," said Duris, "my father gave one of our slaves his freedom. He had served us well, and was more like a friend than a slave. When he received his freedom he was the happiest man I ever saw.

"What is your new slave to do?" he added.

"He is to help my father in his studio," replied Hiero. "I heard Cimon say that he was a vase-maker by trade."

"Let us go into the studio and see him," suggested Duris.

"That is a good plan," responded Hiero. "Perhaps he will teach us how to make vases. That would be fun." And away the boys ran to the studio to form the acquaintance of the new slave.

CHAPTER XII

PREPARING TO BE SOLDIERS

"What is the meaning of all these?" asked Duris, pointing to a large number of bronze pillars, which he and Hiero were passing as they walked along one of the streets of the city.

"Oh," replied Hiero, "those contain the names of the men of Athens who would have to serve in the army, if there should be war. See," he added, going close to one of the pillars, "you can read the names plainly.

"Every year," continued Hiero, "a new pillar is put up, and the oldest one is taken away. That is because a new class from the gymnasium has reached the age of eighteen, and is ready for service. The youths in this class are called *ephebi*. The men whose names are on the oldest pillar are then too old to serve, and their pillar is taken down. There are forty-two pillars in all.

"It is almost time for a new pillar to be set up. The youths are being drilled every day in the gymnasium. Shall we go and watch them?"

"Yes, I should like to," replied Duris, so Philo

and Theron followed, as the boys turned toward the gymnasium.

The gymnasium, like the wrestling school, was built around a court, in which the young men exercised and drilled. Seats were provided for visitors.

"Do you see the tall man with the rod?" asked Hiero, after he and Duris had taken their places. "He has charge of the gymnasium and it is his business to keep order. He does not hesitate to use his rod if there is any trouble. Visitors are just as likely to feel the rod as any one else, if they are not well behaved."

"I see, you are warning me," laughed Duris. "I shall try to be as quiet as a girl," and he folded his hands and looked so solemn that Hiero laughed outright.

The boys found the gymnasium an interesting place. They watched the young men as they practised fencing, spear throwing, and shooting with bow and arrow. But, best of all, they enjoyed seeing them ride, for the horses were spirited, and it required skill to mount and handle them. No saddles were used and no stirrups. A blanket took the place of a saddle, and the rider placed the end of his spear upon the ground and leaped to the horse's back.

As a group of riders dashed past the boys, Duris exclaimed: "They look just like the sculptures on the Parthenon!"

"Yes," said Hiero, "there are many figures of youths on horseback in the Parthenon."

"Who is the man in the midst of that group of youths?" asked Duris, as he and Hiero were about to leave the gymnasium.

"That," said Hiero, "is Socrates, the philosopher. He teaches a class of young men here every day."

As the boys passed the group they heard Socrates saying earnestly, "It is better to be honest than to make sacrifices to the gods."

"My cousin's name is on the last pillar," Hiero said on the way home. "After he had finished his training in the gymnasium there was a great feast at his home. His hair had been cut short, and for the first time he put on the chlamys, which men alone may wear. I am glad we boys wear only the chiton. We are so much more free to run and jump and exercise.

"But, I suppose," he added, "that when we are eighteen, we will be glad to wear the chlamys, for that will show that we are men."

It was not many days after this that Hermippos said to the boys, "The new ephebi take the oath of allegiance to the state, to-morrow. I suppose you would like to go to the theatre and see them."

"Yes, indeed," answered the boys together.

The theatre consisted of row after row of stone seats rising in a semicircle about an open space which served as a stage. There was no covering over the seats or stage, but all was open to the sky.

When Hiero and Duris took their places, it seemed to them that all the citizens of Athens must be in the theatre.

"What a lot of people!" exclaimed Duris.

"Yes," said Hiero, and then he added, "Here come the ephebi."

The young men, with hair cut short and wearing the chlamys or cloak, marched upon the stage of the theatre and their names were written in the records of Athens. Then followed what, to them, seemed the most important part of the ceremony, for each one was given a shield and a spear. As they marched out, each one wearing his shield and carrying his spear, they bore themselves proudly, and the air was filled with the shouts and the applause of the people.

"Now they are soldiers!" said Hiero eagerly.

"What will they do now?" asked Duris.

"They will have to serve for a year in the country outside of Athens. They will ride and march, and go into camp, just as the soldiers do. But after that they will come back to Athens and take part in all the processions and celebrations. It must be fine!"

"But suppose there should be war?" questioned Duris.

"Then they would have to go into battle," said Hiero. "But there have been no wars since Pericles has been our ruler. And there is not likely to be soon, for he has made a treaty of peace which is to last for thirty years. The treaty is called the 'Peace of Pericles.'"

CHAPTER XIII

A Story in the Studio

"Will your father care if we visit the studio?" Duris asked one day, as he and Hiero came in from school.

"No," answered Hiero, "he always likes to have us there."

"My father told me that he had a new group of statues almost finished, and he wanted me to see it."

The two boy entered the studio where Hermippos was at work. The new slave was mixing clay for a model.

"Well," said Hermippos, "have you come to take another lesson in vase making?"

"Not to-day," answered Duris, "but Father wanted me to see your new group of statues."

"It is nearly finished," said Hermippos. "If you boys will wait a few minutes we will have a talk about it."

The boys seated themselves near the slave and watched him as he handled the clay, moistening and kneading it, so that it would be firm and elastic when Hermippos should be ready for it.

In a few minutes Hermippos stepped down from

the platform upon which he had been working. "Now, then," he called to the boys, "come and tell me what you think it represents."

There were three figures in the group, and the boys looked at it earnestly.

"One man," began Hiero slowly, "seems to be a captive. Another is about to kill him. The third man runs toward them,—but I cannot think what story it represents."

"Is it from history?" asked Duris.

"Yes," replied Hermippos, "this group represents an event in the history of Greece, and, of course, there is a story connected with it. It is the story of Damon and Pythias.

"At the time of the story, Dionysius was ruler of a certain city, but he was cruel and unjust. Pythias was one of the citizens and he formed a conspiracy to overthrow Dionysius. However, Dionysius learned of the conspiracy and he captured Pythias and put him in prison. 'You have but a few days to live,' said Dionysius, 'so put your affairs in order. In a short time you shall pay with your life for the conspiracy against me.'

"Now Pythias had some important business to attend to, and he was very much troubled about it. But he had a friend, Damon, who, he knew, would stand by him no matter what trouble he might be in.

"It was not long before Damon came to the prison to see him. Then Pythias told him of all these matters. 'I must see to them,' he said, 'before Dionysius puts an end to my life!'

"'I will willingly stay in the prison in your stead,' volunteered Damon.

"So Dionysius was told that Damon would remain in the prison while Pythias settled his business affairs.

"Dionysius was amazed.

"'I never heard of such friendship as this!' he exclaimed. 'Suppose your friend Pythias does not return?'

"'I will take his place,' said Damon simply, 'but I have no fear that he will not return.'

"Dionysius laughed. 'Do as you will,' he said, 'but I am sure no friendship will stand such a test as that.'

"So Pythias was released from prison.

"Days passed, and the time had almost come when Pythias was to be put to death. Dionysius appeared and laughed again at Damon. 'You will pay with your life for such a friendship,' he declared.

"'He will yet come,' said Damon simply, and just then there was a shout.

"Pythias had been detained, but now he was in sight, running with breathless speed.

"Then the soldier rushed in and told Dionysius that Pythias was at the door of the prison.

"'I order the execution stopped,' shouted Dionysius. 'Such friendship as this between men is too seldom seen. I, myself, would like to be admitted to such a friendship.'

"So Pythias was released, and he and Damon went away from the prison free men."

As Hermippos finished his story he noticed how the eyes of the boys shone, and unconsciously they had clasped each other's hand.

CHAPTER XIV

Duris Leaves Athens

The great music hall which Phorion had built was finished. It was a beautiful building, and Phorion was honored and praised and feasted.

Pericles, the ruler, wished him to make his home in Athens. But there was work in the Island which Phorion had promised to do upon his return there.

"I should be glad to make Athens my home," he said, in talking with Hermippos, "for it is a beautiful city in which to live. But I must fulfill my promise first. Perhaps after that I may return with my family."

"I sincerely hope so," replied Hermippos. "Athens needs men like you. It will be hard for the boys to part." he added.

"I am sure of that," replied Phorion. "I should be glad to take Hiero with me, if I were sure that we could return soon. The boys would enjoy the trip together. But I shall have to stay for some time in the Island, and, besides, I have recently heard rumors of trouble which I like not."

"Ah," said Hermippos, "so you have heard the rumors,

too! I fear that the thirty-year treaty of peace is likely to be broken."

"I am sorry if it is so," replied Phorion. "Pericles is a wise and just ruler. He has made Athens a wonderful city. We must beseech the gods to avert the threatened war."

"It would put an end to the building of temples and the carving of statues," said Hermippos. "But the walls of Athens are too high and too strong for her citizens to feel much fear."

"Here are the boys," he added, as Hiero and Duris came into the room, each with a honey cake in his hand.

"Where did you get the cakes?" asked Phorion.

"Oh, we bought them of a street vender, on our way from school," answered Duris. "We first watched them baked, and they were hot when we bought them."

"Eat your cakes together then," said Phorion with a smile; and then he added, "You boys know, of course, that the music hall is finished, and that we shall soon leave Athens."

The boys exchanged a troubled look.

"Will you be sorry to go?" asked Phorion.

"I shall be very sorry to leave Hiero," Duris replied quickly. "But, of course, our home is in the Island."

"Will we ever see each other again?" asked Hiero soberly.

"No one can answer that question," replied Hermippos. "But we hope it will not be long before Phorion will return with his family, and make his home in Athens."

"Oh!" exclaimed the boys together. "That will be fine."

"When do we leave, Father?" inquired Duris.

"In three days," replied Phorion, "so make the most of your time together."

The next two days were crowded as full as possible with fun and frolic and sightseeing. Toward night of the second day the boys paid a last visit to the Acropolis.

They wandered about the temples, looked at the carvings and statues, and then, standing together by the wall, they looked off to the blue waters of the Mediterranean.

"To-morrow," said Hiero very soberly, "you will be sailing on the water. Athens will seem lonely to me without you."

"I shall miss you, too," said Duris, "but—well, we'll remember the story your father told us about Damon and Pythias—and I hope I can come back to Athens sometime."

"Oh, Duris!" shouted Hiero the next morning, running into the court, where Duris was playing with the pet hare, "Father says that we are going as far as the Piraeus with you."

"Good! Good!" exclaimed Duris. "Then you will see us sail!"

A little later quite a company of people set out from the home of Hermippos on their way to the Piraeus.

Hermippos and Phorion, Hiero and Duris, were each mounted upon a donkey. With them was a large group of slaves. Those belonging to Phorion carried bundles of clothing, blankets and cooking utensils, as they had when they came to Athens. Besides these, they carried bundles in which were many beautiful and costly gifts which Phorion had received while in Athens. Some of these were gifts from Pericles.

"It is nearly two years since you came to Athens," said Hiero as he rode beside Duris.

"Yes," said Duris. "What a lot of things I shall have to tell the boys in the Island. It will be great fun; but I wish you could be with me."

It was not long before they came in sight of the seas, lying blue and sparkling in the morning sun; and soon they had reached the Piraeus.

They rode through the streets of the town, and Hiero noticed how broad and smooth and regular they were compared with the streets of Athens.

"I don't care for such streets at all," he declared loyally. "They are like a sum in arithmetic. The streets of Athens are like a poem."

Phorion and Hermippos laughed, but Phorion added: "There is some truth in what he says. 'Tis plain to be seen that he loves Athens."

When the party reached the dock they dismounted and left the donkeys in care of the slaves.

"We will go on board the triremes," Hermippos said to Hiero. "I think you will enjoy that."

"Oh, yes, indeed!" exclaimed Hiero. "I have always wanted to see what the inside of a ship was like."

All along the docks were boat-houses in which were kept the triremes belonging to the navy of Athens.

"It must be a fine sight when a whole fleet of vessels are on the water!" exclaimed Hiero.

"Yes," replied his father, "it is; but we will hope that it may be many years before Athens finds it necessary to unlock her boat-houses."

The trireme upon which Phorion and Duris were to sail was fastened to one of the docks and they went on board. The boys were soon exploring every part of the ship. But that which interested them most was the place occupied by the men who used the oars. Three rows of seats extended the length of the ship on each side.

Beside each seat was an opening through which the oar extended into the water.

"Now we must leave the ship," said Hermippos, "for the captain is ready to sail."

There were a few hurried words of farewell, Hermippos and Hiero sprang to the dock, the long oars touched the water together, and Phorion and Duris had started upon their homeward journey.

At just about the time that Hermippos and Hiero, with their attendant company of slaves, again entered the gates of Athens, Duris, on board the ship, pointed back to the land and, turning to his father, exclaimed, "See the gleam, Father. The sun is shining upon the Acropolis and touching the tip of Athene's spear."

CHAPTER XV

THE BEGINNING OF WAR

"Father," said Hiero, as he came in from school one day, "the boys at school are talking of nothing but war these days. How is it? I thought that Pericles had made a treaty of peace which was to last for thirty years. Only half that time has passed since the treaty was signed."

"There is such a treaty," answered Hermippos, "though treaties are sometimes broken. I trust that this one will not be, but Athens must defend her honor.

"We cannot see Athens insulted," continued Hermippos, "but war is a terrible thing. It always brings sorrow and trouble and ruin somewhere."

"I had thought it would be rather fine to have a war," said Hiero slowly. "We are taught at school to honor heroes, and to be prepared to defend our city and our country with our lives."

"That is true," replied Hermippos earnestly. "We should honor all who are brave and noble, and try to acquit ourselves bravely and nobly. We should not fear death, even, in a just cause, and all men despise a coward.

"But although war is often necessary, and brave men are needed when a nation's honor is at stake, do not let the excitement or the trappings of war make you forget the fact that war itself is terrible.

"I would not have you a coward, my son," Hermippos concluded, "but I would have you reasonable and just and peaceable when peace does not involve dishonor."

But Hermippos' hope of peace was not to be fulfilled. It was only a few days later when word was brought to Athens that the truce had already been broken and the King of Sparta with his army was marching toward Athens.

Then there was a hurried mustering of soldiers. Pericles sent messengers through all the surrounding country, bidding the farmers leave their fields and their crops and hasten to the city for protection.

"The walls of Athens are strong and high, and they reach to the coast," declared Pericles. "No army can break through them. Our ships can bring supplies to the Piraeus, so all who are within the walls will be safe."

The farmers came from all the country around, bringing their families and camping in the open spaces of the city, or between the walls which led to the Piraeus.

Soon the King of Sparta came with his thousands of soldiers, far outmatching the Athenians in number. They marched across the country, burning the buildings and the stacked grain of the deserted farms.

Inside the walls the people prayed to the gods and wept as they watched the smoke from their ruined homes.

"How strange the city seems," said Hiero, as he went through the streets with Hermippos. "Not at all as it was when Duris and I ran about together."

They passed a group evidently from a farm. The man, with folded arms, marched back and forth. His wife stood screaming and the children, huddled, were beside her, some crying, and all looking toward a black column of smoke.

"See!" cried the man, stopping short in his walk and addressing Hermippos. "That is my farm that is burning. And here we are penned up like rats while the Spartan army destroys our homes. Why cannot we go out and fight like men?"

"Alas," said Hermippos, "we are too few to meet such an army. If Pericles were to open the city gates we should all be captured or slain. Inside the walls we are safe. It is hard, I know," he added, "but think of your wife and children."

That night Hermippos came home with news. "Pericles has decided to send out a fleet of vessels. We will fight along the coast."

"We!" cried Harmonia. "Are you going?"

"Yes," replied Hermippos. "I am going."

In a few days the fleet sailed. Harmonia was a brave woman, but she wept as she bade Hermippos farewell. Helen and Chloris clung to his hands as though they could not let him go.

Hiero felt strangely choked, but he was proud of his father. He remembered his words: "Brave men are needed when a country's honor is at stake: but war is terrible."

Hiero was beginning to understand.

Each day, after the fleet had sailed, he went to the market-place to learn what news there might be, and then he returned to Harmonia and his sisters.

"The Spartan army will not stay much longer," he reported, after one of these visits. "They see that we could stay forever inside the walls of Athens and they could not touch us. They are getting tired of this sort of warfare."

"And will they go away, and will Father come back?" asked Chloris, looking at her mother.

"I hope so," answered Harmonia.

A few days later Hiero returned with better news still. "The Spartan army is making preparations to leave," he cried. "They are taking down their tents, and, in the distance, one company can be seen marching away."

"I hope this will end the war," said Harmonia earnestly.

But the next time Hiero returned from the market-place he came slowly, and when Harmonia saw his face she exclaimed, "What is it, Hiero? What is the news?"

Then he told her that the fleet which Pericles had sent out had been defeated in one of its battles and many of the soldiers had been killed.

"Was that all that you learned?" Harmonia asked, and Hiero answered, "Yes."

At the end of the year a solemn procession was seen, for the citizens of Athens were on the way to the public burial given in honor of those who had been killed in battle.

Among the number was Hiero, who walked proudly, and yet with bowed head, for his father was one of those who had given his life for his country.

The people gathered quietly and reverently about the monuments of the heroes of Athens. Not far away was the Acropolis, and the great statue of Athene, holding with one hand her shield and spear, and in the other the Winged Victory.

Hiero could remember but little afterward of the sacrifices and the ceremonies, but when Pericles spoke in honor of the heroes Hiero listened well, and part of Pericles' words he remembered as long as he lived.

"Let us who remain," said Pericles, "follow their example. Look around on this glorious city, think of her mighty empire. Let the love of her beauty sink into your souls, and when you consider her greatness remember that it was by the daring deeds of her citizens, done in the cause of duty and honor, that she was raised to this glorious height."

Hiero raised his eyes to the Acropolis. His father's statues were upon its greatest temple: his father's life had been given for Athens.

He went home proudly to Harmonia. His heart was sad, but comforted.

CHAPTER XVI

HIERO THE VICTOR

The time for the Olympic festival had come. Truce-bearers, wearing olive wreaths, and carrying herald's staves, went through all the streets of Greece. They proclaimed that the sacred games in honor of Zeus were soon to begin: that for three months war must cease. They invited all citizens of Greece to come to Olympia and witness the contests.

There was great joy in Athens when the truce-hearers arrived. Every one who possibly could made preparations to go to Olympia. All were glad that for three months, at least, there was to be no war.

"The truce-bearers have come," called Hiero, excitedly, as he reached home from the market-place, where the news had been proclaimed.

Harmonia, Helen and Chloris listened eagerly. "Now you will leave us," said Harmonia, "but you will do your best in the races, and I trust you may win the victory. Remember your father, my son. If you win you will add great honor to his name, as well as to your own."

For many months Hiero had been training eagerly and faithfully, for he was at last to enter the running race for boys at Olympia. A few days later he left Athens with a company of men and boys, his trainers, and others who were to take part in the games.

It was a pleasant journey in spite of a hot sun and dusty roads, for they stopped often under the trees to eat, or to dash into a stream for a cooling bath. They marched to the music of the cithara, or to the chorus of a song in which they all joined.

Others were added to their number as they went on, until, as they drew near to Olympia, they formed a great company. Among them were people from every station of life. Peasants and fishermen, poets and statesmen—all were bound for the great festival. Many were on foot, others rode horses, some drove in chariots. When they reached the river they found it covered with rich barges carrying wealthy merchants and high officials from distant states.

"I have never seen such a splendid gathering of people!" exclaimed Hiero to one of his companions. "Nor I," replied the boy. "Even the Panathenaea seems a quiet affair compared with this."

When they reached Olympia those who were to take part in the contests were placed in the care of the rulers of the Olympic games. They were examined and questioned, to make sure that they were fitted by birth and training to enter the races.

When Hiero was asked his parentage he replied proudly, "I am the son of Hermippos, the sculptor, and of Harmonia, of the house of Solon."

After all had been examined, a sacrifice was offered, and each one solemnly promised to use no unfair means to win the contests.

"I am glad the foot races come first," said Hiero to one of his companions. "I should be too anxious to enjoy the other contests, if ours came last."

Early in the morning the rulers of the games, clothed in purple robes, and wearing garlands upon their heads, marched to the stadium, or open space in which the contests were to take place. They were followed by the boys who were to compete in the running race.

As Hiero glanced about him he felt almost dizzy at the sea of faces that rose upon all sides of the stadium.

Then he heard the herald announcing the running race, and he turned quickly away from the vast throng of people in order that he might give all his thought to the contest that was before him.

Soon he heard his own name called by the herald, "Hiero, son of Hermippos, of the city of Athens." Then, as Hiero stepped forward, the challenge rang out, "Has any one here a charge to make against this youth? Has he committed any action unworthy of a competitor in the sacred games of the Olympian Zeus?"

There was no response as the voice of the herald died away, and Hiero stepped back to his place.

At length all was ready, and the boys drew up in line for the race. The signal was given, and they sped away, each one trying his utmost to follow the teaching of his trainer; to attain the greatest speed without waste of strength.

On down the course they sped, and the people shouted and cheered, sprang upon their seats and waved their arms, as the favorite of one group and then another forged ahead of his competitors.

As they neared the end one after another of the racers fell back. Others, who had saved their strength, dashed forward. There was a moment's stillness over all the vast throng of people, then—one boy had touched the goal.

"Hiero! Hiero! Son of Hermippos, of Athens!" rang the cry; and the people clapped their hands and cheered and shouted.

For a moment Hiero struggled for breath, then he drew himself up gladly and proudly, as he realized that the honor of the race was his, and that it was his name that the people were shouting.

Beside the head ruler of the games stood a beautiful tripod of gold and ivory. Upon this tripod were laid the olive wreaths with which the victors were crowned as soon as their contests were over.

The branches from which these crowns were made had been freshly cut from the sacred olive tree. The cutting of the branches was done with a golden sword by a boy of pure Greek birth, both of whose parents were living.

This boy, with the golden sword in his hand, now stood beside the tripod.

Hiero was the first victor.

As the herald called his name he stepped before the chief ruler and bowed his head to receive the victor's wreath.

What a thrill of joy and pride passed over him as he felt its touch!

He lifted his head—then he started! He looked straight into the eyes of the boy who carried the golden sword, and the boy was—Duris!

Once more the people cheered and shouted, but for the moment Hiero forgot the crowd and the cheering. His hands were clasped in those of Duris, and the fatherly arm that lay across his shoulders was that of Phorion, his father's friend.

"You are victor once more!" cried Duris. And then he added, "We are going now to Athens to live."

"We can return together then!" exclaimed Hiero. "Oh! I am glad!"

But they had time to say no more, for the people were throwing garlands and flowers and gifts at Hiero's feet.

Flushed and proud and happy, he bowed to right and left as he gathered up his treasures, and when his arms overflowed it was Phorion who stepped to his side to help him.

During the remaining days of the festival Hiero and Duris spent most of the time together. They sang together the hymns of victory, they marched side by side in the processions, and they feasted at the same banquets.

But it was on the long march back to Athens that they had the most time in which to tell of all that had happened during their time of separation.

At length the triumphal procession drew near the city. "Athens!" exclaimed Hiero, and Duris added: "The city that we both love!"

Hiero's heart beat fast. "How glad my mother and sisters will be," he thought, and a great happiness surged over him.

"For The Moment Hiero Forgot The Crowd And The Cheering."

As they entered the city gates there was music and singing and joyous laughter.

"Ah," exclaimed Duris, "how proud I am! It is good to return to Athens by the side of 'Hiero the Victor.'"

THE END.